ACADEMY

READY FOR ACTION

TOY ACADEMY

READY FOR ACTION

BRIAN LYNCH

ILLUSTRATED BY EDWARDIAN TAYLOR

SCHOLASTIC INC.

To Mom, Dad, and Christina. Thanks for making me me. —B.L.

To Jamey and my mini wolf pack: Samurai, Jinx,

Hansel & Gretel. —E.T.

• • •

ISBN 978-1-338-54165-6

10 9 8 7 6 5 4 3 2 1   19 20 21 22 23

Printed in the U.S.A.   40
First printing 2019

Book design by Mary Claire Cruz and Keirsten Geise

CHAPTER ONE
TITAN BREACH MEMOIRS

The action figure had been kept in the display case of the Titan Toys lobby for years. Her name was **TEMPEST BOOMCLOUD**, and she was stuck in a glass box next to other discontinued toys, across from a TV that played an endless loop of cartoons based on Titan Toys properties.

Tempest knew every line to every show. She had their theme songs buzzing around her head 24/7. It was downright unbearable. And just when she thought things couldn't get any worse, the humans put up a sign in the lobby . . .

CRYIN' LION

TEMPEST BOOMCLOUD

BOT-BOT

CELEBRATING **25** YEARS OF

ELITE ACTION FORCE NOW

PARTY IN TITAN TOYS CAFETERIA IN 2 DAYS. DRESS AS YOUR FAVORITE MEMBER OF THE TEAM.

Tempest couldn't take it anymore. She used her battle glove to tear through her packaging.

"Where are you going?" Cryin' Lion asked.

"Far away from the likes of you!" Tempest barked.

Cryin' Lion started crying, to absolutely no one's surprise. Tempest ignored the sobs and boldly kicked open the glass door. But she also lost her balance, fell from her shelf, and landed on the floor.

The noise alerted one of the Titan Toys guards. He came running in search of the source of the noise. Tempest raised her battle glove and made a fist, ready to battle with the large human. If she was going to be found out, she wasn't going down without a fight.

Luckily, Tempest didn't have to battle. She didn't have to do anything. The watchman didn't see her. He simply closed the display case and left. Tempest had been **IGNORED YET AGAIN.**

This time, she took advantage of it. She ran out the front door.

Tempest Boomcloud was a free toy.

Now she had to find a way to Toy World, where her mission could truly begin.

By the time she was finished, every toy would know her name.

CHAPTER TWO
FURRY ROAD

In the human world, the **ELITE ACTION FORCE NOW** toys were super popular playthings. But here in Toy World, they protected civilians from threats of all shapes, sizes, and toy lines. To celebrate Elite Action Force Now's twenty-fifth anniversary, Toy World was throwing an Anniversary Parade of Greatness. It would begin at the Knickknack Valley clock tower and end at Toy Academy. There would be balloons, floats, and musical numbers (but no fireworks because most of the citizens of Toy World were flammable).

The Toy Academy students were excited about the parade, and even more excited that they'd have the day off from school. But for now, class was in session, so the plushes were learning how to cuddle, water toys learned bathtub basics, and action figures were making glorious use of the school's racetrack.

Grumbolt's Road Ripper tore down the track, zigzagging around dozens of other toy vehicles. He sped past a tank, an armored jeep, and a rhino on wheels. Up ahead he spotted the triple loop-de-loop.

"You're gonna wreck the car!" Rex Everything yelled as he pulled up in his **REX VAN**. Rex was the lead character of the Elite Action Force Now toy line. He was also a bully. He only liked two things: himself and his Rex Van.

"Leave me alone!" Grumbolt yelled. "Go bother someone else!"

The loop-de-loop loomed over him. Grumbolt's mind started to race. Was Rex correct? Was he going to crash? Those loops *did* look scary. The cotton in Grumbolt's stomach began to swirl.

His friend Micro pulled up on the other side of Grumbolt.

"Ignore Rex!" Micro yelled. "Hit max speed and the velocity will take care of the rest! You can do this!"

Micro knew what she was talking about. She was a toy historian and the smartest toy Grumbolt knew.

He revved the engine and shot up the first loop. *Yesss! He had done it.* As he was taking the second, he saw Rex in his rearview mirror. Rex was driving with one hand, which left the other hand free to point and laugh at Grumbolt. Grumbolt felt the

cotton in his stomach start to expand even more.
His foot dropped off the gas.

The Road Ripper dropped off the second loop.

Grumbolt smashed to the ground.

Rex laughed so hard that he lost control of his
Rex Van and crashed right next to him.

CHAPTER THREE
THE GRUM OF ALL FEARS

"Are you ready?" Professor Goldhawk asked with a smile.

Everyone in Fighting 201 was anxious to see which accessories Goldhawk had picked for them to spar with. They had just finished mastering the water pistols and sponge swords of the H2Oh-No: Water Fighters! toy line. Grumbolt was glad they were done with those, as every Water Fighters accessory sprayed water or shot bubbles and that really did a number on his cloth exterior.

Goldhawk opened a large collector's case, and the students got excited.

They'd be using **BOOSTER ARMOR**.

"Booster Armor gives you new powers and enhances your natural abilities, so be careful," Professor Goldhawk explained. "Everyone find armor that fits your mold."

Micro found her armor and immediately lifted her classmate Tank Face above her head like it was nothing. "Check it out! My back-of-the-box file card *strength levels* now match my back-of-the-box file card *intelligence levels*!"

Grumbolt dug through the pile, but he couldn't find any armor that fit. Everything was made for taller, stronger molded plastic figures, not hastily made, home-sewn dolls. Micro took him by the paw. "I know one suit of armor that'll fit you."

Sure enough, she did. It was a Veggie Warriors original. Veggie Warriors were a discontinued line of toys intended to make vegetables cool for kids. It did not work out. Grumbolt fit right into their Broccoli Armor, or, as it was called on the box, the official Rich in Iron Man costume.

Grumbolt sighed. Micro thought it was because he was dressed as broccoli, which would dampen any toy's spirit. But it wasn't just that: Grumbolt was still hung up on his failure at the racetrack. "Maybe I should go back to being a plush," he said. "Go back to hugging and whatnot."

"What?" Micro couldn't believe her ears.

"I crashed!" Grumbolt explained. "I thought I could do those loops—I was ready! But then Rex got in my head and I messed up. We have to drive those loops again tomorrow, and the thought is making me feel sick. Action figures aren't supposed to be scared! Maybe . . . maybe Commander Hedgehog was just being nice when he let me switch majors."

Micro shook her head. "Grumbolt, Commander Hedgehog let you switch majors because you saved Toy Academy!"

Tank Face leaned over and interjected, "Yes, but almost *everyone* here has saved Toy Academy."

She wasn't wrong. Toy Academy had *many* hero toys, and that meant lots of villain toys came looking for them. The school was a magnet for daily **TOY BATTLES,** or **TOY RACES** to the **TOY DEATH,** or at the very least **HEATED TOY DISAGREEMENTS.**

"Grumbolt got lucky and saved the school once!" Rex Everything laughed. "It doesn't mean he's an action figure! Stuffed toys are never tough."

Micro whispered, "What about **TEDDY BEARS**?"

Rex's eyes widened. "Don't bring them up! They'll hear you and they'll come!"

"What's so scary about Teddy Bears?" Grumbolt asked. "I saw some in a toy store. They seem cuddly."

"Oh, they like to cuddle all right," Micro said. "They *live* to hug and squeeze. Which is fine if you're a giant human, but here in Toy World? Those monstrous beasts crush anything they get their paws on. They're kept in the highest security area of the Playville Zoo, behind thick plastic doors. So, yes, Rex. Stuffed animals CAN be tough."

"W-w-what do you know?" Rex stammered. "You're barely an action figure yourself!"

Grumbolt had had enough. It was one thing to put him down, but it was another thing entirely to insult his best friend. It's true, Micro began her career at Toy Academy as a collectable. But then she also switched her major to action, and she was doing great.

"I'll have you know," Grumbolt announced, "Micro gets straight As in every class!"

"Not every class," Micro said. "Not since I changed majors."

"She gets straight As in MOST classes!" Grumbolt declared.

"Getting mostly Bs," Micro mumbled.

Grumbolt shrugged. "Micro is getting the letter closest to A in every class! Besides, remember when she just lifted Tank Face above her head? That was crazy."

"That was the Booster Armor," Rex shot back. "The minute she takes it off, she's back to being a loser."

Rex walked away, satisfied that he had made all parties feel rotten.

CHAPTER FOUR
SIDEKICKED

The action figures were told to report to Toy Academy's foosball field for Intro to Rescues. There, standing with their teacher, Professor Rescuesaurus, was the founder of the school, Commander Hedgehog.

"Students," Commander Hedgehog said. "A few years back, I was the lead character on an animated show. By my side for every single episode was my junior partner, **ENSIGN MOLE RAT**."

"Ensign Mole Rat is the coolest!" Micro said.

HE CAME PACKAGED WITH COMMANDER HEDGEHOG!

HE STOOD NEXT TO COMMANDER HEDGEHOG!

HE CARRIED COMMANDER HEDGEHOG'S WEAPONS!

"Technically the second coolest. Mole Rat is my **SIDEKICK**," the commander continued. "Working with a sidekick, or working *as* a side-kick, is a vital part of being an action figure.

"I will randomly assign each of you a partner. For the next month, you will work with him or her every day. At the end of the month, you and your partner will run an obstacle course featuring some of the toughest playsets you've ever seen. The **PLAYSET OBSTACLE COURSE** will be divided into three sections: Rescue, Battle, and Driving. How you do on the course will account for one-quarter of your grade."

"I've been waiting for this day forever!" Micro whispered. "I hope I get Punchy for my sidekick!"

Punchy was a strong, scrappy boxing figure.

Micro clapped her hands. "This could turn things around! This could really help my grade!"

"You're getting Bs!" Grumbolt whispered. "I'd love to get even one B."

"I just . . . I know I can be the best," Micro said. "I want to see straight As on my report card! With a powerhouse like Punchy on my side, it could happen!"

"Time to announce sidekicks!" the commander declared. "Micro Gigantic, your sidekick is **KEY BEE**."

A tiny plastic bee made her way through the crowd. She was super small. Made of flimsy rubber. She looked like she was barely an action figure at all.

In fact . . .

Key Bee had a tiny chain coming out of her back. At the end of the chain was a giant silver loop.

Micro's sidekick wasn't a toy at all.

Micro had been paired with a **KEYCHAIN**.

CHAPTER FIVE

NOT TO BEE

"Hi! So happy to be here and working with you!" Key Bee exclaimed.

"*Really* excited about this!" Micro said, lying. "And just to be clear, you are a keychain, right?"

"You bet I am!" Key Bee cheered. "I love keys. Pin keys, lever lock keys, car keys, giant novelty keys. I also *love*, *love*, *love* locks. Padlocks, dead bolts . . . "

Micro nodded politely, but then blurted out, "But is a keychain an action figure?"

"She has an action feature," Commander Hedgehog said.

Key Bee demonstrated. A blinding light shined from her stinger.

"Oh, how nice. Your butt glows." Micro sighed.

Grumbolt noticed the expression on Micro's face was getting more and more pained. He figured a change of subject might help. Plus, he was really excited to meet *his* new partner.

"Where's my sidekick?" Grumbolt asked. He had a feeling he was going to be assigned someone really cool.

"Grumbolt . . . you're not the main hero type," Commander Hedgehog explained. "You'd be sold in the package *with* a figure, along with the hero's weapon and hat."

"*I'm* the sidekick?" Grumbolt gulped. "Really? So who's my hero?"

Commander Hedgehog didn't know quite how to say it.

"Who is it?" Grumbolt asked. "I can take it."

Commander Hedgehog couldn't even look at him.

"YOU'RE THE SIDEKICK TO REX EVERYTHING."

"No way!" Rex insisted. "Watch the *Elite Action Force Now* cartoon. We're too cool for stupid animal sidekicks!"

"*Elite Action Force Now*," Grumbolt moaned. "So lame."

"Why don't I take your cotton butt to the **PARADE IN OUR HONOR** and you can call my team lame to their chiseled faces," Rex said. "I'll drive you myself, just hop in the Rex Van's trunk-jail, and let's go."

"Maybe your *van* should be your sidekick." Grumbolt laughed. "After all, it *is* your best friend."

"That's right it's my best friend!" Rex yelled. "It has turrets and an ejector seat and it can fly, like a good friend should."

"Boys, you are partners," Commander Hedgehog declared. "Find a way to make this work."

Grumbolt knew, plain and simple, that this just *couldn't* work. Rex was mean. And he hated Grumbolt. Together, Grumbolt and Rex would most certainly fail the Playset Obstacle Course.

CHAPTER SIX
WATCH AND LEARN

Micro told Grumbolt to meet her in Toy Academy's viewing-room playset. There, she and Key Bee were loading the DVD player. Key Bee looked . . . different.

"Micro helped me look more like an action figure," Key Bee said. "What do you think? I'm not so sure."

"You look great!" Micro said. "Now, on to your problem, Grumbolt. You're stuck with Rex Everything, so you'd better learn everything about him. We're gonna watch episodes of the *Elite Action Force Now* cartoon."

The idea of spending his night watching Rex's adventures seemed like torture. But Grumbolt quickly discovered that the *Elite Action Force Now* cartoon was actually pretty great. The soldiers of Elite Action Force Now had cool weapons and vehicles, and the show had a super catchy theme song:

Get into your battle vehicle,
Drive into the fight!
Grab the weapon for the job,
Defend what's just and right!
Activate your action feature,
Now you'll be the best!
Earn the badge of heroism,
Wear it on your vest!
The enemy's tough, but you're tougher!
The going gets rough, but you're rougher!
The world will know your story!
You will get your glory!
Elite Action Force Nowwwww!

Grumbolt had to admit, there was a lot to like about the Rex Everything in the cartoon. He was brave, kind, and noble.

Grumbolt turned to Micro and Key Bee. "Wow, can you believe that?"

"Yeah!" Key Bee exclaimed. "In that first episode, the ninja left his car door unlocked! And then in episode four, the vault had a European lock but that biker man picked it like it was a typical American cylinder!"

"Right, I totally noticed that," Grumbolt said. (He didn't.) "Also, the Rex on the show is nothing like the Rex that goes to school with us."

Micro nodded. "Rex Everything figures are usually good guys. The best guys, really. And Elite Action Force Now cadets usually train at their own headquarters, not at Toy Academy."

"Why wasn't our Rex sent there to learn?" Grumbolt asked. "Why does Toy Academy have to put up with him?"

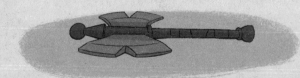

"Maybe Rex was sent to Toy Academy to learn to be nicer," Key Bee said. "Maybe the potential to be nice is in there. You just have to help unlock it."

Grumbolt thought about it. Maybe Rex *could* be nice. Maybe if Grumbolt was a great sidekick, Rex could become a great hero.

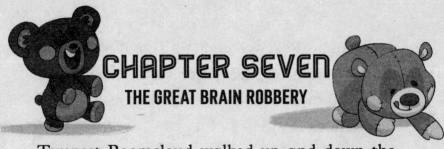

CHAPTER SEVEN
THE GREAT BRAIN ROBBERY

Tempest Boomcloud walked up and down the aisles of Atomic Hank's Toy Store. She was searching for a fabled playset that allowed for travel between the human world and Toy World. And while she was at it, she asked each and every toy the same question:

"DO YOU KNOW WHO I AM?"

None of them did. Not even Super Genius Margie.

"Here's a hint," Tempest said, "my name is Tempest Boomcloud. Does that strike fear and/or admiration into your hearts?"

The toys stared at her, confused. A bin of Teddy Bears, however, were very excited to see her. They reached for Tempest, desperate to get to her. Tempest beamed as she walked toward the bears. "Finally somebody knows me!"

"Stop!" a tiny voice yelled from the discount section of the store. "Those bears will hug you to death!"

Tempest backed away from the bears and headed toward the voice. There, among the unwanted playthings of days gone past, sandwiched between the Veggie Warriors and Librarian Squad toys, was a tiny robot named BRAINO.

"That was close!" Braino said. "Teddy Bears will crush anything they can get their paws on!"

Tempest looked the robot up and down. "Your box says you are the world's smartest toy, is that true?"

"Yes, I'm a learning toy," Braino responded sadly. "But I was returned by three different kids. I have no idea why."

Your artistic talent is lacking.

"I'm sorry for your situation," Tempest said. "I know what it's like to be thrown away. But rest assured, **THE WORLD WILL KNOW YOU.**"

Tempest used her battle glove to tear through Braino's packaging. Braino hurried out and hugged her. "Thank you! Oh, thank you! I can never repay you!"

"You can and you will," Tempest responded. "Use that beautiful giant brain of yours to find me a Warp Zone playset."

"Oh, that's easy!" Braino said, pointing to the store's one Warp Zone, hidden deep in the discount section behind a bunch of square basketballs.

"Good." Tempest nodded. "We're going to Toy World. Once we're there, and this is very important, I need you to FIND ME A REX EVERYTHING VAN."

CHAPTER EIGHT
NEXT TO REX

Grumbolt did his best to be a great sidekick to Rex Everything. He carried all of Rex's accessories for him. He held the door for Rex everywhere they went, and announced Rex's arrival each time. He even hummed the *Elite Action Force Now* theme song as Rex walked. During their Saving the Day for Beginners class, Grumbolt took notes for Rex so Rex could draw pictures of his battle van.

"Say my archvillain, Labrador Deceiver, wants to steal the ancient Scratching Post of Knowledge," Professor Calico De Claw said. "What's the most creative and fun way to stop him?"

Micro's hand shot into the air. "Set a classic bait and switch trap! Put the Scratching Post on a big red X. Labrador Deceiver says, *HA HA HA HA, YOU THINK YOU FOOLED ME?* He steps to the side of it, but OH NO, now he's standing on a net, which springs up and snatches him! Boom! In your face, Labrador Deceiver!"

Key Bee cheered. Rex wasn't as impressed. "Any villain worth their sticker price is gonna be able to break through a net. You gotta use a cage that drops out of nowhere right on them!"

"And then, when Labrador Deceiver is caught," Grumbolt added, "a big sign could pop up that says, *Sorry for the Cage, I Hope You Use This Time to Self-Reflect.*"

"You're the worst," Rex said, shaking his head. Grumbolt was frustrated, but he was not about to be deterred. Rex must have good in him somewhere.

CHAPTER NINE
THE CLASS AND THE FURIOUS

Micro told Grumbolt and Rex to meet her at the racetrack at lunch. "Ever since Rex messed with him and caused him to crash, Grumbolt has been nervous about this part of the sidekick obstacle course. So I figured we'd better deal with it head-on."

Grumbolt could feel the cotton in his belly swirl. "Oh, boy. The loops again."

"Yeah, they're scary," Key Bee agreed.

"If you're gonna be action figures, you gotta get over your fears," Micro said. "And Rex, they're our partners. We don't make them feel bad, we help them. Heroes, get in the driver's seat for now; sidekicks, you ride passenger."

Grumbolt climbed into Rex's battle van.

"Don't sit down," Rex said, not looking at him. "I don't want your loser butt on the van's upholstery. Just hover."

Grumbolt did his best to comply.

Micro shot up the track and Rex pulled in behind her. They were fast approaching the first loop.

"I'm not frightened!" Grumbolt yelled, covering his eyes.

"Okay!" Micro barked. "Sidekicks take the wheel!"

Grumbolt had to take over MID-LOOP? He was going to crash again. The cotton in his belly began to swirl.

"You can do it!" Micro yelled.

Grumbolt nodded, took a deep breath, and put his paws on the wheel.

"Not happening." Rex sneered. "This van is only to be driven by the leader of Elite Action Force Now! It says so in the instruction manual! Besides, you can't do the loops! YOU CAN'T DO ANYTHING!"

Rex's words hit Grumbolt like a ton of bricks. Grumbolt's paws started shaking; he lost control of the Rex Van, which shot off the track . . .

. . . flew through the air . . .

. . . and landed in a plastic tree.

"Are you okay?" Rex cried as he and Grumbolt stumbled out.

"Yeah, I'm—I'm all right," Grumbolt stammered.

"I was asking my van!" Rex barked, checking to see if any of the Rex Van's stickers had ripped in the crash. "Look what you did! Grumbolt, you are the worst!"

Grumbolt had tried all day to be supportive of Rex in an attempt to find Rex's good side. But the truth was becoming clear:

Rex Everything didn't have a good side.

Just then, the wind picked up.

Flying over them was a toy they had never seen before.

"Greetings, Toy Academy!" the figure yelled.
"Prepare to be invaded by Tempest Boomcloud!"

CHAPTER TEN
VAN ON THE RUN

Micro turned to Key Bee. "You need to run."

"Okay, run right at her?" Key Bee asked. "I'll do it!"

"No, run *away*!" Micro said. "Go hide!"

"But she's a bad guy, right? I can help," Key Bee offered.

"I appreciate that," Micro shot back. "And if this were playtime, I'd let you pretend to be a hero. But this is real. And you're just a—"

"Keychain?" Key Bee said sadly.

"Exactly!" Micro responded, opening the Rex Van's trunk-jail. "Hide here; it's armored and it triple locks!"

Key Bee fluttered her tiny wings and got in the trunk. "I'll do it because I'm your sidekick and I have to do what you say, but—"

Micro gave her the thumbs-up and slammed the trunk door as Tempest approached.

"**DO YOU KNOW WHO I AM?**" Tempest asked.

Grumbolt, Micro, and Rex looked at one another, confused. An annoyed Tempest clenched her fist, but then Micro said, "Your build is familiar."

Tempest lowered her fist. "Go on."

Micro looked Tempest up and down. "Joint placement, articulation, your battle grip . . . Holy cow, you're an Elite Action Force Now figure!"

Tempest smiled.

"This nut is from my toy line?" Rex asked. "I've never seen her."

The smile dropped from Tempest's face. "No, you haven't. I never made it to production. Titan Toys locked me away in a cabinet of misfits. Away from the action, forced to live next to a TV that played the theme song to the show I was supposed to *star in*, over and over again! That was bad enough, but then I hear Elite Action Force Now is getting an anniversary party."

"Yup," Rex bragged. "Toy World is throwing a parade to celebrate its favorite heroes tomorrow."

"You're no heroes!" Tempest yelled. "Heroes don't let toys *from their own line* gather dust for decades in plastic cases! You should have rescued me!"

"Why would Elite Action Force Now save a villain toy?" Rex said.

"You're naive," Tempest replied as she went to open the Rex Van's door. Rex blocked her.

"I'm not here to fight." Tempest sighed. "I snuck an angry puffer fish bath toy into Toy Academy's pool so your greatest warrior, Commander Hedgehog, would be dealing with that during my visit. Just let me take the van and I'll leave."

Rex didn't budge. "You will never, never take my van."

"I don't *want* to fight." Tempest smiled. "It doesn't mean I *won't*."

Rex tapped his shoulder button, activating his **REX-IN-EFFECT** action feature. His leg shot up toward Tempest. She blocked the strike with cold ease. He retaliated with a Rex punch. She raised a hand toward him. His fist **CRUNCHED** against her open palm.

"Ow!" Rex said. "You're *durable*."

He threw another punch. This one landed on her shoulder. And this one hurt him even more.

"You're cheating! You're not made of normal plastic! It's like punching a brick wall!" Rex whimpered.

Growing tired of the battle, Tempest upper-cut him with her battle glove. Rex was down.

Micro stepped up, raised her fists.

"Braino?" Tempest asked, pointing to Micro.

Braino looked Micro over.

No accessories. Scared look on her face. She won't be a problem.

"Rude!" was all Micro could get out before Tempest took her down, too.

All that remained was Grumbolt. He wanted to help. He wanted to fight. But he just stood there, too scared to act. Tempest even gave him a few moments to try something, but he didn't budge.

"Maybe next time?" Tempest laughed. "Braino, **GET INTO MY BATTLE VEHICLE!**"

Tempest and Braino climbed into the Rex Van. A rocket booster extended from the van's bumper and wings popped out from either side.

The Rex Van was airborne.

"Wait! Key Bee's in there!" Micro leaped for the van, but it was already too high.

Tempest wasn't done yet. She spun the vehicle toward Rex.

"THE ENEMY'S TOUGH." She smiled.

"BUT I'M TOUGHER."

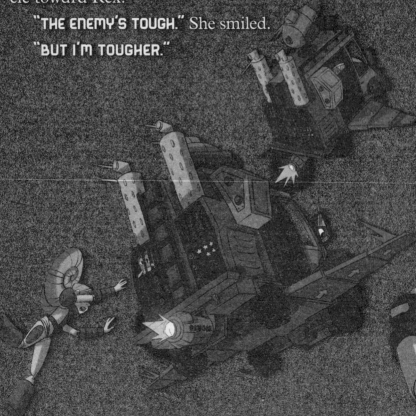

Tempest hit the gas. The Rex Van hurled toward Rex. *The very thing he loved the most was about to be used against him.*

The army man dove for cover, but Grumbolt just stood there, too scared to move.

"Hold on!" a gruff but reassuring voice boomed. OmniBus Squared, the school's head of security, rushed over and shielded Grumbolt with his body. The van smashed into OmniBus, and OmniBus's metal body crunched on impact.

"On to the next mission!" Tempest yelled. "See you at the parade!"

The Rex Van rocketed away from Toy Academy.

Tempest Boomcloud was gone, and she had taken Key Bee with her.

CHAPTER ELEVEN
AFTER THE TEMPEST

The students gave their description of Tempest to Cupcake Unicorn, Playville's police sketch artist. Commander Hedgehog stormed in and demanded to know what had happened. Micro told him all about Tempest Boomcloud. He studied Cupcake Unicorn's sketch of Tempest.

"Is this accurate?" Commander Hedgehog asked his students.

Micro shook her head. "At no point did she did say that. Also, she didn't have hearts in her eyes."

Commander Hedgehog used his Adventure-Screen to call General Elite, the founder of Elite Action Force Now.

"Very busy, Hedgehog," General Elite said. "We're preparing for the big parade to celebrate the wonderfulness that is us."

"Fantastic," Commander Hedgehog said, rolling his eyes. "We had an attack on Toy Academy grounds today."

"Did Rex Everything handle it?" General Elite asked hopefully.

"No, sir," Rex replied sheepishly.

The general shot him a dirty look, before muttering, "Big surprise."

Commander Hedgehog continued. "Right, well, it seems to be an enemy of Elite Action Force Now. And she's coming for you during your **ANNIVERSARY PARADE OF GREATNESS**."

"So let her!" General Elite laughed. "We have lots of archenemies and villain toys threatening to try and take us down during our parade! We're looking forward to it! The crowd will love it!"

"She took a student of ours," Commander Hedgehog said. There was no reaction. So he added, *"And one of your vans."*

General Elite got deadly serious. "Why didn't you say so? We'll handle this."

The screen cut to static.

"I'm going to help them," Micro said.

"You're forbidden to go after Tempest," the commander snapped. "It's for your own good. You're first-year figures. Don't worry, OmniBus Squared and I will help them bring Tempest to justice. Let's go, old friend!"

OmniBus stood up and tried to transform. But midway through, he froze. Stuck in a form that was not quite robot, not quite bus.

"OmniBus?" the commander asked.

"I'm trying!" OmniBus said. "But I took a real hit from that Rex Van. Did some damage. I . . . I MAY NEVER TRANSFORM AGAIN."

CHAPTER TWELVE
BEE FREE

Tempest landed the Rex Van in an abandoned barn playset in Plastic Grove Farmlands.

"Is this our new secret lair?" Braino asked excitedly.

"No. It's temporary," Tempest responded.

Suddenly, the trunk popped open.

Key Bee fluttered out, scared as can be. Tempest grabbed her by the chain.

"Trying to follow me, hmmmmm?" Tempest laughed.

"No ma'am!" Key Bee responded. "My hero told me to hide on account of she thought I couldn't be useful!"

"Boss, that bee just broke out of a triple-locked trunk-jail!" Braino gasped.

"I-I-I'm sorry. I'm good with locks."

Tempest thought about this for a moment. Then she pulled the keychain close and looked at her, eye to eye. "Whoever told you that you couldn't be useful is a fool."

Key Bee was surprised. It was the nicest thing anyone had said to her in a while, and it was said by the villain who had kidnapped her.

Tempest smiled at her new friend/prisoner. "Let's put you to the test."

CHAPTER THIRTEEN
QUEST FOOT FORWARD

Grumbolt and Micro sat on the stoop of Castle Fort Lair in silence.

Grumbolt felt terrible. OmniBus had been injured protecting him, because Grumbolt was too scared to do anything.

"Why did I tell Key Bee to hide in the van?" Micro said, shaking her head. "I'm the worst."

Rex stopped in front of them. "At least you didn't let some lame evil figure steal your battle vehicle. By the way, Grumbolt, Micro lost her stupid sidekick. I didn't. Carry my books."

He shoved his books into Grumbolt's paws. Grumbolt looked down at the book on top.

"A **QUEST**," Grumbolt said to himself.

"Is that what it says?" Rex shrugged. "I don't take that class, I just bought it because it's the biggest book and I thought it'd be funny to see you carry it."

The book gave Grumbolt an idea. "Micro, we should go on a quest! Find Tempest, stop her, and get back what she took! I can prove I'm a real action figure! You can rescue Key Bee!"

Micro lit up. This was a good idea.

"And I can lead the quest," Rex said. "I can defeat Tempest Boomcloud and get my van back."

"You weren't invited—" Grumbolt said.

"I'm your hero, you're my sidekick," Rex argued. "Commander Hedgehog said so."

Thus, it was decided. Grumbolt and Micro were going to defy Commander Hedgehog's orders to stay away from Tempest. They were going to find Tempest, and they were going to bring her in. And Rex Everything was going with them, because nothing can ever go 100 percent right.

CHAPTER FOURTEEN
BAD THEFT AUTO

Grumbolt ran back to his dorm room. His roommate, Paper Dave, was there. He could not know about Grumbolt's secret mission.

"Hey, roomie!" Grumbolt said. "Just doing normal stuff, no quests for this guy."

Grumbolt grabbed his backpack with the intention to fill it with the most action-y things in his room. But what to bring? The only accessory he had was a plastic shield he found on top of a trash can.

No, wait, upon further inspection, it was the *lid* to a trash can. Still, he couldn't show up for the quest empty-pawed . . . so he grabbed the trash can lid and threw it in his backpack. For good measure, he tossed in a ball of yarn to give the bag some weight.

Grumbolt headed outside, where Rex was waiting with a giant bag.

"All my accessories," Rex said. "You're carrying them."

"Okay, fine," Grumbolt said, before patting his backpack. "Lots of cool stuff in here, too. Trust me."

"Let's do this!" Micro burst out of the dorms. She, too, had prepared for the quest, in her own special way.

"Hey, Tempest is made of superplastic. She's tough. We might need a little more power," she explained.

"You look ridiculous," Rex scoffed.

Micro ripped a plastic tree out from its roots and held it above her head.

Rex nodded. "Fine, whatever. Let's go find a battle vehicle and hit the road."

They headed to Toy Academy's garage to borrow a battle vehicle for their mission. The Ultra Rocket looked perfect.

"Don't worry," Micro said. "I have an eleven-point plan to get it."

1. SNEAK IN.
2. DO SOME RECON.
3. TRANSCRIBE RECON RESULTS.
4. ANALYZE RECON RESULTS.
5. DOUBLE-CHECK RECON
   RESULTS.

Around point five, Micro realized that Micro was losing her audience.

"Wait, no, I have a cooler plan," Micro said.

1. SNEAK IN.
2. LIFT THE ULTRA ROCKET OVER MY
   HEAD WITH MY INCREDIBLE NEW
   BOOSTER ARMOR.

Rex interrupted. "That's not what we're doing. My plan is better."

1. KICK THE DOOR OPEN.
2. KICK WHOEVER'S THERE.
3. HEROICALLY STEAL THE
   ULTRA ROCKET.

"Guys," Grumbolt said, "I took half a semester of drama class under the tutelage of Professor Drama Pig, who taught me about the art of camouflage. I have a plan."

1. PUT ON INCREDIBLE DISGUISE.
2. SNEAK IN AND BORROW THE ULTRA
   ROCKET.
3. RETURN IT LATER, BETTER THAN
   IT WAS, WITH NEW PAINT JOB AND
   STICKERS, SO EVERYONE'S GLAD WE
   TOOK IT.

All three toys thought their plan was best. So they all tried their plans at once.

Rex kicked the door open.

Micro lifted the Ultra Rocket.

Grumbolt disguised himself.

At that moment, OmniBus Squared entered the garage. Micro quickly put the Ultra Rocket down and hid under it. Rex dove behind the fruit-scented Razberry Chariot. Grumbolt stood perfectly still to remain hidden.

"Hello, Grumbolt," OmniBus said.

"Hi!" Grumbolt replied, surprised that the old robot saw through the disguise. "What are you doing here?"

"I was waddling by when the garage's alarm went off," OmniBus explained. "I looked in the window and thought I saw someone lifting a car above her head. I came in to check it out, but I guess I was wrong. I've been a little confused since the accident. What *are* you doing in that terrible disguise, by the way?"

The stuffing in Grumbolt's belly began to churn. He was going to be found out and get detention or *worse*. He stood there in awkward nervous silence.

OmniBus sighed. "Yeah, I'm flustered, too, after Tempest's attack. You're not gonna do anything crazy, like go find Tempest, are you?"

Again, Grumbolt was unsure of his next move. So he just stared at OmniBus, a confused expression on his face.

"Silly of me to ask," OmniBus said. "But

what are you doing here? Did you want to prac-
tice your driving?"

How was he supposed to answer that? He didn't
want to lie! Grumbolt just shrugged and said,
"Uh . . . uh . . . "

OmniBus nodded. "Okay, go ahead and sign
a car out."

Grumbolt was confused. He was going to get
a battle vehicle? Wow, his plan was *so* good, *so*
subtle that even *he* hadn't known about it! He
was going to steal the best vehicle right under
OmniBus's nose! Grumbolt strutted toward the
Ultra Rocket.

"No, no, no!" OmniBus said. "You've been crashing a lot lately. Take . . . this one."

And that is how Grumbolt got his team the official Veggie Warriors Cob Car.

CHAPTER FIFTEEN
CORN TO RIDE

OmniBus left Grumbolt to get acquainted with his horrible car. Grumbolt slid into the driver's seat as Rex and Micro came out of hiding.

"This is perfect!" Micro cheered. "No one will notice us because the minute anyone sees a Veggie Warriors toy, they avert their eyes."

"I deserve something better!" Rex yelled. "I get the *best* battle vehicle! It's in my theme song!"

Grumbolt nodded excitedly. "You're darn right it is!" Truth be told, he'd had the incredible *Elite Action Force Now* song running through his head since he had heard it the night before.

"Get into your battle vehicle! Drive into the fight!" Grumbolt sang.

"Okay, enough . . . " Rex said.

But it *wasn't* enough. Grumbolt kept going. "Grab the weapon for the job! Defend what's just and right!"

"Stop!" Rex roared. Grumbolt ignored his request, and jumped to his favorite line.

"The enemy's tough, but you're tougher!"

"Nobody can be tough in a giant ear of corn!" Rex insisted.

"What'd you just say?" Micro said.

"I said it's a giant ear of corn," Rex grumbled.

"No," Micro said. "*The enemy's tough, but you're tougher.* Tempest said that to us, right before she left."

Grumbolt's button eyes widened.

"Tempest Boomcloud was trapped in a display case hearing that song over and over!" Micro said. "What if the *Elite Action Force Now* theme song is **PROVIDING A BLUEPRINT FOR HER REVENGE**? The first line started with, *Get into your battle vehicle*, so she stole one."

"And when she gets to the end of the song . . ." Rex said.

"The world will know her story! She will get her glory," Grumbolt sang.

"She thinks she's owed everything," Rex said. "So she's gonna take it all."

"But if we know the next line, we know what she's doing next, right?" Micro asked.

"Grab the weapon for the job!" Grumbolt sang.

"Hey, yeah, she doesn't have any accessories."

"Only one place to go for the best weapons," Micro said. "Grumbolt, get this corn to the Playville Museum of Rare and Discontinued Accessories."

CHAPTER SIXTEEN
MISTAKEOUT

Grumbolt parked the Cob Car across the street from the Playville Museum of Rare and Discontinued Accessories. It was late, so the museum was closed.

"Now we wait for Tempest to show her face," Rex said.

"This is exciting!" Micro blurted. "I thought I wasn't going to be on a stakeout until Stakeouts 101 in my sophomore year, and even then it would have been a simulation."

"What do we do on stakeouts?" Grumbolt asked.

Rex got out his binoculars and watched the front door. "We keep our eyes on the doors and windows."

Micro leaned forward. "Actually, I've read the Stakeout textbook already. While we wait, we're all supposed to bond by talking about personal stuff."

"You've already read next year's textbooks?" Grumbolt asked. "You are awesome!"

Grumbolt raised his hand to high-five.

"We'd better not," Micro said. "My Booster Armor increases my strength far too much; a high five from me would be more like a high two hundred, and I just don't think you're built to withstand that."

"Armor or no, you're still a nerd, Micro," Rex grumbled.

Micro looked hurt. Grumbolt didn't like Rex insulting his friend like that, so he tried a little passive-aggressive retaliation. "Tell us something personal, Rex. For instance, maybe you can tell us why you were sent to Toy Academy instead of training at Point Elite like the rest of your toy line."

Rex glared at Grumbolt for a good couple of minutes. He only stopped when a stuffed elephant arrived at the museum, clutching a delivery box.

The elephant went inside and shut the door.

"Should we have interrogated the stuffed elephant?" Grumbolt asked. "We could do good toy, bad cop."

Micro leaned forward in her seat. "Actually, fun fact: That wasn't a stuffed elephant. It was a 1982 Halloween costume for a Zookeeper Margie."

"That fact wasn't fun at all!" Rex barked.

Grumbolt turned to Micro. "Wait, that was a costume?"

"It was . . . " Micro jumped out of the car. "That could have been Tempest!"

Rex followed her and marched toward the museum. Grumbolt hurried behind him.

"All right, showtime!" Rex declared.

"So this is it, huh?" Grumbolt said, starting to get nervous. "We're actually gonna do this? O-okay, great . . . "

Rex kicked the front door of the museum. It didn't budge.

"Let me try," Micro said. She grabbed the knob and accidentally ripped the door off its hinges.

"Oops," she said. "Still getting the hang of the Booster Armor."

Rex and Micro ran in. Grumbolt took a deep breath, counted to five, realized he was stalling because he was scared, counted to five again, took another deep breath, and ran in.

Guards were tied up in rubber bands. And sure enough, the elephant disguise was off and under it was no Zookeeper Margie.

Tempest Boomcloud had snuck into the museum.

"The jig is up, Boomcloud!" Micro yelled. "Where's Key Bee?"

"She's fine," Tempest responded calmly. "She's with Braino. And as for the jig . . . "

Tempest smashed a display case and picked up an intimidating accessory.

"It's very much *down*."

"The Elite Action Force Now Hypno-Staff!" Micro said. "It was made for the *leader* of Elite Action Force Now. Rumor has it, it can hypnotize any toy! It was never mass-produced because it's too powerful!"

Tempest sighed. "It was never mass-produced because it's a choking hazard. And it was made for *me*."

"Yeah, right," Rex scoffed.

"Yeah, right," Tempest said as she held the staff high. "Because I am the true leader of Elite Action Force Now."

CHAPTER SEVENTEEN
THE SECRET ORIGIN OF TEMPEST BOOMCLOUD

"This discontinued nerd is talking crazy," Rex said. "I'm the leader of Elite Action Force Now."

"You are the leader of Elite Action Force Now *now*," Tempest shot back. "But at the dawn of the toy line, plans were different."

TEMPEST BOOMCLOUD

Titan Toys wanted Elite Action Force Now to be led by the coolest, most powerful action figure ever made. I was that figure.

Elite Action Force Now needed a new leader. Titan Toys picked the figure that was supposed to be the team's aerobics instructor.

"That's why you're so tough!" Micro said. "Prototypes are made of ultra-polycarbonate! Superplastic! Super durable for all the tests they have to run!"

"Who cares about that!" Rex yelled. He turned to Tempest. "You're telling me that I was originally an aerobics instructor?"

Tempest nodded. "Your original name was **FLEX EVERYTHING**. Your action feature kick is merely a way to build strong thigh muscles. Titan Toys changed your name and uniform, and you became the figurehead of Elite Action Force Now."

The room was silent. Rex stood perfectly still, his head hung low.

Micro broke the silence. "So, does that Hypno-Staff actually work?"

Tempest nodded proudly. "It can hypnotize any figure."

"Are you gonna use it on Toy World?" Micro asked. "Turn everyone into toy zombies to do your bidding?"

Tempest glared at Micro. "That is a villain plan! **I AM NOT A VILLAIN!** How dare you!"

Now Micro had done it. Tempest went over to a wall of discontinued lawn-dart cannons and started firing at her. Micro hid behind a discontinued Porcupine Mobile. Hiding was definitely a plan Grumbolt could get behind. He dragged Rex behind the Porcupine Mobile with Micro. Lawn darts flew all around them.

"What do we do?" Grumbolt asked.

"I don't know!" Micro said, starting to freak out. "This is too real!"

Grumbolt knew Micro could figure this out, she just had to approach it a different way. "Micro, pretend it's an assignment! Pretend our teacher said there's a *completely harmless* figure firing a *super-fun*, *non-dangerous* weapon at us. We have to defeat that figure to get an A. What do we do?"

Micro grinned: Now Grumbolt was speaking her language. She analyzed the room. "We hit her with that H2Oh-No: Water Fighters! water sprayer at a forty-five-degree angle, and it sends her out that window. But how do we reach the sprayer? It's on the other side of the room!"

There was no way Grumbolt was going to try and run across the room. He figured they had better devise a plan B. "Okay, let's—"

"Throw you across the room?" Micro said excitedly. "Grumbolt, that's genius!"

That was not at all what Grumbolt had in mind. But before Grumbolt had a chance to protest, Micro grabbed him by the arm and chucked him with all her Booster Armor–enhanced might.

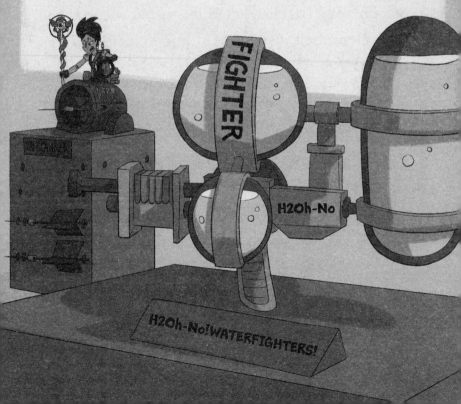

Grumbolt sailed across the room.

He landed near the water sprayer. Grumbolt looked up, and saw a lawn dart about to land directly on top on him. He quickly rolled out of the way, dodged a second dart, and dove for the water sprayer. Tempest aimed the lawn dart cannon at him, just as he aimed the water sprayer at her.

"Hey, is that **TEMPEST BOOMCLOUD**?" Micro yelled, flailing her arms. Tempest, thrilled to be recognized, was distracted for a split second. It gave Grumbolt just enough time to squeeze the trigger.

The water gushed out and smashed into
Tempest, sending her flying through the window.

They ran out of the museum. Tempest was already gone, and now she had the Hypno-Staff. *But* they had survived the encounter, which was a check in the win column.

"Come on, Rex!" Micro yelled as they headed toward the Cob Car.

"The name . . . " Rex sighed. ". . . is Flex. Just leave me here."

"It would make the mission easier," Micro whispered.

Grumbolt reached into his backpack and pulled out the yarn. He wrapped one end around his waist and the other around Rex's. Grumbolt walked toward the Cob Car, pulling Rex along behind him.

"What was the next line of the song?" Micro asked.

Grumbolt belted out, "Activate your action feature!"

"That's right!" Micro nodded. "Tempest is super strong and smart and cooler than Rex, but she doesn't have an action feature. Let's hop in the corn and head to the New & Improved Funtime Sights and Sounds Hospital."

CHAPTER EIGHTEEN
OUR FEATURE PRESENTATION

Micro parked the car. "If you're a toy and you want to change your appearance, this is the place to go. Fresh paint jobs, new bodies, greater articulation, *and* action features."

Grumbolt helped a depressed Rex out and led him toward the playset.

Micro opened the entrance door, accidentally ripping it off its hinges.

"Sorry," she said to no one in particular.

They entered the main lobby and walked up to the receptionist, a teeny, tiny fairy princess.

RECEPTION

"Excuse me," Grumbolt said. "Has an action figure named Tempest Boomcloud been in here recently?"

"We cannot divulge the name of any of our patients."

The fairy princess sounded like a loud pirate. No, she sounded like five pirates. Five angry pirates, all shouting at once.

She could see the confused look on Grumbolt's face, and responded, **"New voice chip. Just one of the many upgrades available at New & Improved."**

Grumbolt thought the fairy princess sounded super tough. Maybe *he* could get a voice chip. A cool, gruff voice would definitely make him seem like more of an action figure.

But why stop there?

"What else do you guys do?" he asked.

"New paint jobs, new body parts, more muscles, less muscles, wings, robot arms, you name it."

The fairy princess handed Grumbolt a business card. He didn't have any place to put it. "Do you also do pockets?"

Micro shook her head. "Grumbolt, you're perfect. Don't change yourself." Grumbolt shot a glance at Micro's Booster Armor, which made her very defensive. "This is just for the quest! But if it goes well, I don't know, I may keep it."

An office door swung open. A Doctor Margie was leaving . . . with Tempest Boomcloud.

"No way!" Tempest barked.

"Did you give that *villain* an action feature?" Micro asked Margie.

"That's confidential!" Doctor Margie stated.

Micro tapped a button on her Booster Armor. "It doesn't matter! Either way, we're stopping her here and now!"

Grumbolt didn't know what to do. Tempest was probably super angry at him for blasting her out the window with the water toy. He wanted to stop her, but he also wanted to hide from her. He split the difference and just stood there. It seemed to be his go-to move lately.

Tempest, however, was on the move. She darted away and ran through the entrance, now doorless thanks to Micro. A valet pulled the Rex Van right up to Tempest.

"Your vehicle's modifications have been made!" the valet said happily. He tapped the steering wheel, which made the van declare:

TEMPEST
BOOMCLOUD
IS THE BEST

"She . . . she . . . " Rex stuttered.

Grumbolt couldn't believe it. Rex was finally talking.

"She . . . gave it a new sound feature?"

"She took it to a Mechanic Margie in the New & Improved garage," Doctor Margie said sheepishly.

Tempest zoomed away in the Rex Van.

"*She* didn't get an action feature!" Micro declared. "She gave the van one!"

"She made my van **DECLARE ITS LOVE FOR HER?** Unacceptable!" Rex yelled.

"You're darn right it is!" Grumbolt said.

Rex smiled at Grumbolt, thankful for the backup. Then he slung Grumbolt over his shoulder.

"Wait a minute!" was all Grumbolt could say as Rex ran after his van.

Grumbolt had to admit, he was impressed that Rex was running as fast as a battle vehicle. Rex's humble beginning as aerobics instructor Flex Everything was seriously paying off. Rex was almost to his van; he could just about touch it . . .

. . . when Tempest activated the van's flying feature for a quick escape.

Rex screamed into the air. "Tempest Boomcloud is *not* the true leader of Elite Action Force Now! I am! No more moping, we are catching her! You and me, hero and sidekick!"

Rex glanced at Grumbolt for a second and then looked away. "And thanks for not leaving me before or whatever."

Grumbolt shrugged. "I'm your sidekick."

Doctor Margie pulled up in her Margie Race Car. Micro got out of the passenger seat. "Of all the action features you could give yourself," she said, "kick feature, punch, double-kick, double-punch, double-punch *while* double-kicking, karate chop, spin-slap, hammer smack . . . *Why just alter your van?*"

Grumbolt immediately knew. "She wants somebody to like her. Now the van says it does whenever she hits a button."

"Okay, that's sad. What's the next line in that stupid song?" Micro asked.

"It's not stupid; it's the best song," Grumbolt said. "The next line is: Earn the badge of hero-ism, wear it on your vest! It's the last thing she has to get."

Grumbolt turned to Margie. "Margie dolls can do it all. I know you're a doctor, and it appears you're also a race car driver. But by any chance are you also a star news reporter?"

Doctor Margie smiled. "Of course! Why?"

"Tempest Boomcloud wants a badge," Grumbolt said. "I say we give her one."

CHAPTER NINETEEN
THIS JUST IN

Tempest returned to the abandoned barn. When she entered she was surprised to see multiple TV screens and cages, along with four trapdoors that weren't there when she had left.

"Braino!" she yelled. "Did you turn this into an evil lair?"

Braino had a guilty look on his robot face. "Maybe a little."

"We are not evil! And this barn is not our headquarters!" Tempest barked. "After tomorrow, we'll be able to move into whatever playset we want!"

Tempest noticed a large maze with multiple doors and locks in the corner of the barn. "You built a **DEATH TRAP**?"

"Every evil lair playset has one!" Braino contested. "Also, you said you wanted me to test Key Bee's lock-picking ability. So I constructed a maze with hundreds of doors with impossible locks at every step."

Tempest was intrigued. "And?"

"She beat the maze in seconds. Any lock I throw at her, she can pick. She got out of the maze, and then went back into the maze to go down all the other possible routes and unlock all the doors there!"

Key Bee poked her head out of the maze. "Are you mad?"

"Quite the opposite!" Tempest smiled. "You bested Braino. Let's hope he made up for this failure by locating an Elite Badge of Heroism."

Braino was silent. Tempest stared at him in disbelief. "Not even ONE Elite Badge of Heroism?"

"What about that one on TV?" asked Key Bee.

Tempest looked at one of the monitors, and was shocked by what she saw. Those Toy Academy misfits were being interviewed by Star news reporter Margie.

"I'm here with Rex Everything, the leader of Elite Action Force Now!" Margie said. "Along with his sidekick, Gumball."

Grumbolt raised a paw. "It's Grumbolt."

Margie continued. "Rex, word is you've been dealing with a toy named Tempest Boomcloud?"

"Yeah, but we bested her all day today." Rex laughed.

"WHAT?" Tempest yelled. "Nobody bested me!"

Rex continued, "We did so well, we got an award."

"The rarest, coolest Elite Action Force Now Badge of Heroism ever!" Rex smiled. "Well, time for me and my sidekick to hang out by the big oak in Knickknack Valley Park! I'll be there tonight, completely vulnerable, so nobody come looking for trouble."

Tempest was fuming. Braino turned to her and said, "Boss, this is clearly a trap."

"Ready my battle vehicle!" Tempest yelled. "I am going to get that badge from Rex Everything, and then I'm going to take him apart, piece by piece!"

CHAPTER TWENTY
TRAP BATTLE

Rex stood by the big oak tree in Knickknack Valley Park, clutching his very special garbage can lid. His sidekick, Grumbolt, stood next to him. They tried out a couple of cool poses to assume when Tempest arrived.

THE "LET'S DO THIS."

THE "OH, I DIDN'T SEE YOU THERE."

THE "WHY ARE WE DANCING?"

They saw the Rex Van entering the park and heading right for them. Tempest was behind the wheel. Grumbolt could see that she looked *really mad*. His stomach rumbled, and his paws started shaking.

"Rex," Grumbolt said. "Maybe I should stand behind you. Like way, way behind you, like across the street, how does that sound?"

Rex didn't answer. He was doing his best to look stoic, but his hands were shaking, too.

The van **SCREECHED** to a halt.

"So, Rex, you bested me?" Tempest yelled.

Rex cleared his throat and nodded, before holding up his makeshift Elite Badge of Heroism. "Well, it *would* explain why I have this."

"You lie!" Tempest yelled, taking one more step toward him. But then she noticed she was standing on a bright red X. She laughed at their pathetic attempt at trapping her and stepped off to the side of the X.

"NOW!" Grumbolt yelled.

A confused Tempest barely had any time to act as Micro, well-hidden in the oak tree, dropped a giant cage over Tempest and Braino.

"We were safe until we moved off the X!" Braino deduced. "This trap was multilayered! Actually quite ingenious."

"Thank you!" Micro said. "See, Rex, the *bait and switch* is a hit!"

Rex smiled at her. "Yeah, but it's my cage that is keeping them trapped!"

But the trap wasn't over. A sign popped up.

SORRY
For the Cage.
I Hope you
Use This Time
to
Self-Reflect.

Unfortunately for everyone involved, Tempest was not going to take the sign's advice. She reached through the bars and grabbed Grumbolt with her battle glove. She pulled him close. Grumbolt tried to wriggle free, but Tempest's grip was tight.

"Release me!" Tempest demanded. "Or I will shred this doll."

"Ma'am, I'm a . . . I'm an action figure."

Tempest looked at Grumbolt and laughed. "Then why do I feel like we're cuddling? If your friends don't let me go, I will rip you apart."

Grumbolt was getting more and more nervous by the second. He tried to calm down, he tried to retain his cool, but Tempest was way stronger. Also, she was too honest.

She's wrong. I AM an action figure, Grumbolt thought. *I gotta calm down, I can't freak out, I'm taught to handle this kind of situation at Toy Academy. What would my teachers tell me to do? Do I punch? Karate chop? Should I deliver a moral?*

He was doing his best, but the truth is, Grumbolt was too scared to think clearly. He had no idea what to do next. His friends, however, were ready to help. Micro leaped down from the tree and swung at Tempest. The cage immediately fell apart under Micro's Booster punch.

MICRO HAD JUST FREED TEMPEST.

It was fine, though. Thanks to her Booster Armor, Micro could try again super fast. She delivered another Booster Punch . . .

. . . which Tempest redirected right into Rex's jaw.

"I thought you were supposed to be the smart one?" Tempest smiled as she grabbed the *HERO* garbage can lid.

Tempest darted to the Rex Van. Braino climbed in the passenger seat. The van rocketed away into the night.

Micro ran after her . . .

. . . but she was blocked by a team of Action Force Now toys. And a very, very angry Commander Hedgehog.

CHAPTER TWENTY-ONE
BUSTED TOYS

"I told you students to stay away from Tempest Boomcloud!" Commander Hedgehog yelled.

Micro held her head low. "We were just trying to help."

A gruff voice came from a tank rolling directly behind Commander Hedgehog. "Well, you didn't, at all."

The tank's hatch opened and out climbed General Elite. The other members of Elite Action Force Now filed in behind him. Heroic-looking men and women with muscles on top of muscles. Each and every one clutching the newest, coolest accessories. They were the best and they knew it. *Everybody* knew it.

"It's my team!" Rex said, before nervously tapping his shoulder button, and then waving nervously, finally landing on a proper salute.

"You okay?" Grumbolt asked.

Rex nodded. "I'm great, I'm the best."

"At ease, Everything," General Elite said. "Hedgehog, your students better stop trying to steal our villains. Whatever Tempest Boomcloud has planned for our parade tomorrow, the

greatest soldiers in all of Toy World can handle it. Isn't that right?" General Elite put up his fist.

The members of Elite Action Force Now returned his salute and shouted, "Elite Action Force *and How*," in perfect unison.

"The parade is scheduled to end at your school tomorrow," General Elite continued. "But if these troublemakers will be anywhere near it, maybe we should relocate."

"They're not going to cause a problem," Commander Hedgehog said. "Grumbolt, Micro, Rex Everything, you will report to the Dungeon playset for detention until the celebration is over."

"Well, wait a minute . . . " Elite said. "Not Rex."

Rex perked up. "What did you say?"

General Elite put his arm around Rex. "You broke the rules, but you did finally show **COURAGE**. Plus, you're our lead character, we need you for the parade."

Rex didn't know what to say. He glanced at Grumbolt and Micro.

"I don't know . . . " Rex said. "It doesn't feel, what's the word, *right*."

But the general wasn't done. "We'll also give you a new van. Next year's model. Not in stores yet. More weapons. Louder sounds."

Rex shook his head. "No, sir."

Grumbolt smiled.

"I want **TWO VANS**," Rex said. "One black, one gold."

General Elite nodded, and Rex hurried away from Grumbolt and Micro, back to his old team. He was fist-bumping and yelling, "Elite Action Force *and How*," over and over again.

Grumbolt and Micro's quest was over.

CHAPTER TWENTY-TWO
PLAN BEE

Tempest removed Key Bee's blindfold. It was pitch-black out. Key Bee activated her light-up butt to see an imposing plastic door in front of her. Something on the other side was growling and scraping, desperate to get out.

"I must admit, I didn't know how I was gonna break through this door," Tempest admitted. "I was racking my brain, I was racking Braino's brain, to figure it out. My battle glove, maybe? A few other toys, battering rams, angry gorillas? No idea. But then you flew into my lap. This other toy, forgotten and underappreciated and ready to show the world what she's capable of. You reminded me of a smaller, far less collectable me."

"What's on the other side?" Key Bee asked, scared.

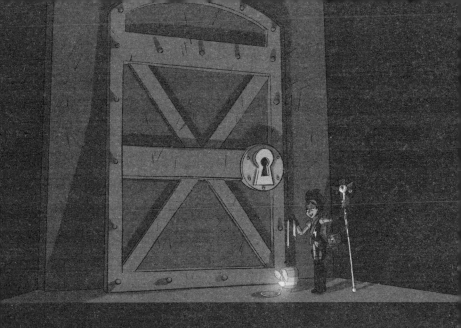

"It doesn't matter," Tempest said. "Just think of this as your final test. You open this door, and I'll keep you safe from any carnage that's coming for Toy World tomorrow."

"And if I refuse?"

Tempest shrugged. "Then I'll use my glove and get a battering ram and an angry gorilla, and I'll get it open. And then I'll throw you in."

Key Bee got to work.

CHAPTER TWENTY-THREE
GRUM KIND OF WONDERFUL

The Dungeon playset was dismal. No windows, no light, just a few wooden desks and plastic stone walls. It was official: Detention stunk. OmniBus sat in the front of the room, watching over Grumbolt and Micro.

Micro was passing the time practicing moves with her Booster Armor. Grumbolt sat slumped in his chair, depressed. He had really wanted the quest to go well. He wanted to save Key Bee. He even wanted to help Rex. But he wasn't made for action. He was just a goofy little stuffed animal. And when push came to shove, **HE JUST WASN'T BRAVE** like all the other action figures.

"I don't care if Rex's team is excited to fight Tempest Boomcloud, we need to get out there!" Micro said. "You think they care about Key Bee? No! She's my sidekick, I have to save her!"

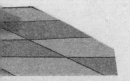

"She's right!" a voice said on the other side of the wall.

Rex Everything kicked open the door. "Our quest isn't over!"

OmniBus stood up with difficulty. "Rex, get back to the parade."

Rex held up a toolbox. "OmniBus, if you let these two nerds go, you're gonna get fixed."

OmniBus wasn't having it. "The smartest toys in Toy World couldn't repair me!"

"Actually," Rex said, "the smartest one hasn't tried yet."

Rex kicked the toolbox across the floor. It stopped at Micro's feet.

"That dork is the smartest dork on this entire dork planet," Rex said. "She fixes you, you let us go, we stop Tempest."

"Why do you want to do it?" Micro asked. "*You're back on your actual team.*"

"No, I'm not!" Rex yelled. "*This* is my team!"

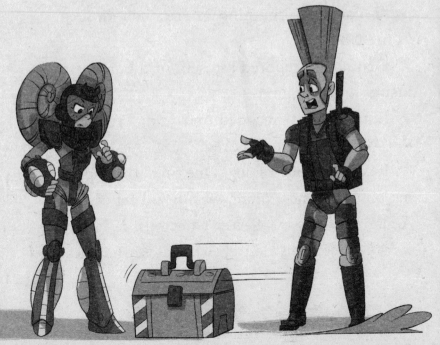

Grumbolt thought about it. "You don't like the new van."

"I don't, at all," Rex said. "Either one. I got a black one and a gold one, and they're both terrible. The seats are different. The sounds are too loud. I want my old van back. And to do that I need to defeat Tempest, but I'm feeling generous so I'm letting you help me."

Micro smiled. "In."

Rex looked to Grumbolt.

"No."

Rex looked at Grumbolt, confused.

"I can't do anything," Grumbolt argued. "I'm **SCARED**."

Grumbolt prepared himself for a barrage of insults and laughing.

But Rex just shrugged and said, "Yeah, me too. Who doesn't get scared?"

Rex took a deep sigh. "One time, this kid got me on Christmas, along with a full set of Elite Action Force Now Series One toys. When he went to sleep, his dog chewed each and every figure. Except for me . . . because I hid. Well, General Elite heard about it. Sent me to Toy Academy. He said I had to learn how to stop only caring about myself. But when I was hiding from that dog, it wasn't because I was selfish, it was because I was scared."

Grumbolt looked at Rex . . .

. . . and a huge grin broke out over his face.

"I shouldn't have said anything," Rex said. "Forget I said it, that was just a test and you failed."

Grumbolt stood up. "Everybody's scared!"

"I don't know about that . . . " OmniBus said.

"Oh, please!" Micro laughed. "Highflyer? He's a toy glider but he's afraid of heights! That's why he only flies two inches off the ground. He would literally be higher if he stood up and walked."

"Future Cop?" Rex added. "He gets gassy every time he's about to fight. He says *power wind* is his action feature."

OmniBus shrugged. "I agreed to monitor detention because I was afraid of anyone seeing me like this."

Grumbolt looked to Micro. "What about you?"

"Oh, not me. I'm the exception that proves the rule," Micro replied. "Well, I'm a little scared about not being the best. Like, it keeps me up at night, and consumes my every thought. But other than that, I'm great."

"All this time," Grumbolt said, "I thought I was awful because I got nervous. Because the cotton stuffing swirled in my belly. But now I realize that everybody is scared! **NOBODY HAS THEIR STUFFING TOGETHER!**"

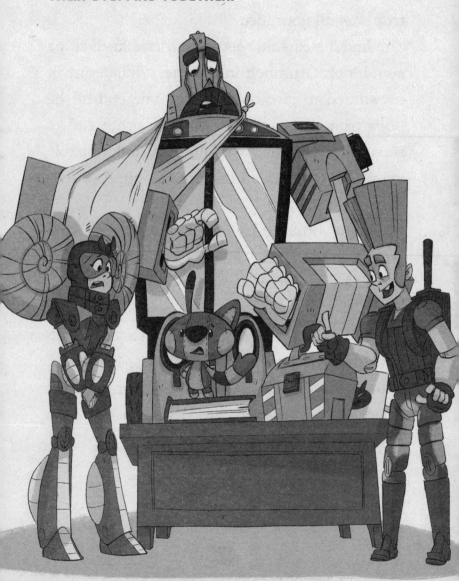

"Also, not for nothing," Micro said. "Scared or not, you did score us a car. And shoot Tempest out the window with a water squirter. And the trap was all your idea."

"And," Rex said, getting on one knee so he could look Grumbolt in the eye. "When one of us wanted to give up, you tied one end of the yarn around your waist and the other end of the yarn around his way more muscular, heroic waist and you made him come along. And that was very cool."

Micro flung off her Booster Armor and picked up the tools. "What? I can't very well fix OmniBus with that stupid armor on."

"We're gonna need some help," Rex said. "Elite Action Force Now is busy, so let's reach out to all the other action toy lines. If it kicks, transforms, lights up, or has a spring-loaded anything, we need it here ASAP to help stop whatever Tempest has planned."

"Good luck with that." OmniBus chuckled. "Most of the action toy lines are investigating the stolen bears."

Grumbolt looked at the old robot. "What are you talking about?"

OmniBus shrugged. "Some weirdo stole all the savage Teddy Bears from the Playville Zoo."

Grumbolt's eyes widened.

Micro looked up.

And Rex did his best to look like he also knew what they had figured out.

Grumbolt got that sick feeling in his belly again. "Tempest Boomcloud is going to unleash the Teddy Bears."

CHAPTER TWENTY-FOUR
BEAR IT

The big day had arrived. Hundreds of toy citizens, along with Toy Academy's students and faculty, marched in the parade behind General Elite and the members of Elite Action Force Now, finally ending up at Toy Academy.

"Elite Action Force Now risks life, limb, and paint job to make sure the citizens of Toy World can sleep at night," President Space Lincoln proclaimed. "Thank you, Elite Action Force Now, and here's to twenty-five more years!"

General Elite posed in an action stance. "We'll be here for you! From assembly line to discount bin, we will protect Toy World from anything thrown its way!"

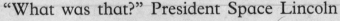

The ground trembled beneath their feet.

"What was that?" President Space Lincoln asked.

"Relax!" the general said, putting his hands on his hips. "Whatever it is, it's no match for us!"

Another quake. This one bigger. Some of the older toys lost their balance and fell over. Battle vehicle car alarms went off in the distance.

Grumbolt, Micro, and Rex ran to the podium.

"Students!" Commander Hedgehog yelled from the crowd. "I told you to stay in detention!"

Another quake, this one bigger still. The science building toppled.

"Sir, we came to warn you!" Micro yelled. "We have to get everyone out of here!"

But before she could finish, there was another giant shudder.

The toys parted to make way for a figure clutching the Hypno-Staff high.

It was Braino. And behind him was every Teddy Bear from the Playville Zoo.

"Citizens of Toy World!" Braino announced. "My army of Teddy Bears is here to destroy you all!"

"*Braino's* army?" Grumbolt asked Micro. "What happened to Tempest?"

But there was no time to figure it out. Braino turned off the Hypno-Staff.

The bears instantly snapped out of their trance. They were awake and aware and they **WANTED TO HUG**. They hugged anything that moved . . . and anything that didn't. They scooped vehicles, playsets, and buildings alike in their velvety paws and squeezed them until they crumbled. Commander Hedgehog and the Toy Academy faculty helped usher as many toys as they could into the most durable playset on campus, Castle Fort Lair.

General Elite ran at the bears, accessories raised. It was a noble, dramatic gesture that he

was really hoping everyone noticed. Everyone did. They also noticed a Get Well Soon Bear scoop him up and start hugging him to pieces.

"Grappling gun!" Rex said. Grumbolt was ready. He tossed the accessory to his teammate, who fired it at the Get Well Soon Bear's arm. Rex hit retract, and it yanked him toward the bear. With one perfectly timed *Rex-in-Effect* kick, the general was freed.

Before the Get Well Soon Bear could grab him, Rex dashed down its arm and jumped to the ground. He did his best to free other figures caught in the hugging onslaught. The other Elite Action Force Now figures followed Rex's lead and started to fight back. But they were plastic figures, no match for Teddy Bears' velvet grip.

Just then, a familiar Rex Van shot through the main gates and landed in front of the bears.

"TEMPEST BOOMCLOUD IS THE BEST" the battle vehicle declared at the top of its horn. Tempest Boomcloud leaped out, her Elite Badge of Heroism held high.

"Citizens of Toy World! I am Tempest Boomcloud! Elite Action Force Now has failed you, but I will not!"

Tempest pushed Braino down.

"Ah!" Braino yelled unconvincingly. "I am defeated!"

She swiped the Hypno-Staff from his robot mitts. Tempest smiled. She had written a new role for herself, and **THE WORLD WAS ABOUT TO KNOW HER STORY.**

Before she had a chance to do anything, General Elite ran over and tapped his shoulder button. His *General-Mayhem* action feature activated, and he let loose a flurry of punches that knocked the *HERO* trash can lid out of Tempest's hands. The general grabbed the Hypno-Staff from her clutches . . .

. . . and BROKE IT OVER HIS KNEE.

"The day is saved!" General Elite declared.

"It's the opposite of that, you fool!" Tempest
yelled. "That staff was the only way to subdue
the bears!"

She swung her battle glove–clad fist at General Elite. Someone had to think fast . . .

Luckily, that's what Micro was best at.

She grabbed the *HERO* trash can lid and dove in front of General Elite.

Tempest's fist struck the lid!

The impact sent Micro flying. She smashed against the Rex Van.

Grumbolt was safe, but his best friend was down.

Elite Action Force Now was fighting for their tiny toy lives.

And the bears were just getting started.

CHAPTER TWENTY-FIVE
HUG LIFE

The Rex Van's trunk popped open. Key Bee fluttered out to see Micro trying to stagger to her feet.

"Micro?" Key Bee asked. "Tempest quintuple locked me in the trunk! It took me a while to pick all five locks. What's going on?"

Micro staggered to her feet and pointed at the bears laying waste to Toy Academy. Rex was doing his best to save as many lives as he could, alongside Commander Hedgehog and the remaining members of Elite Action Force Now. But they were getting overwhelmed.

Meanwhile, Tempest was stunned. "I was . . . I was afraid to be forgotten. I . . . wanted my moment," she said. "I wanted to prove I'm better than anyone here."

"You don't prove how good you are by **ATTACKING PEOPLE**," Grumbolt said. "You prove it by **HELPING THEM**."

Tempest glared at Grumbolt. And then, her angry expression softened. Was that weird little doll correct? Was she doing this all wrong?

"So what do I do?" Tempest asked. "Do I fight the bears?"

Grumbolt shook his head. "You're plastic. They'd crush you in a second."

"I'm superplastic," Tempest said. "Slightly more durable."

Grumbolt thought about it. "Okay, so they'd crush you in *two* seconds."

Grumbolt was right. Tempest couldn't handle the bears. She wasn't *made* to hug. None of the action figures on campus were.

BUT HE WAS.

Grumbolt ran over to Key Bee.

"Oh!" Key Bee said. "Hello, Grumbolt!"

"Key Bee, turn on your butt-light!" Grumbolt yelled. "Make it happy-glow, for all the world to see!"

Key Bee activated her light.

"Can you go brighter?" Grumbolt asked.

She turned up the light. Her butt shone bright and proud, and it shone on Grumbolt.

The spotlight attracted the attention of every single Teddy Bear. They zeroed in on the adorable stuffed doll.

"Yo, bears! you want to hug something?"
Grumbolt shouted as he ran to his Cob Car.
"Hug me! I'm soft and cuddly!"

Grumbolt and Key Bee jumped in his car. "Great work," he said. "Keep your butt lit!"

"Will do!" Key Bee said. "But why?"

"I'm going to lead them out of here!" Grumbolt started the car and revved the engine. "Micro, I need a location with no other toys."

Micro thought about it. "The Diorama Desert! It's too hot for most toys but stuffed animals can take it—"

Grumbolt hit the gas. The Cob Car sped through the campus and rocketed away from Toy Academy, the Teddy Bears right behind.

Grumbolt's stomach gurgled and swirled, but he ignored it. There was no time for fear. He quickly programmed the Cob Car's GPS for the quickest route to the Diorama Desert.

"Turn right at the Plastic Grove Farmlands," the GPS instructed him.

"Hang on, Key Bee!" Grumbolt yelled as he made a sharp right. The bears followed. They entered the main town of Playville.

"Left at the battery charging station. Right at the Accessory Mall."

Citizens of Playville watched in awe from the safety of their homes as Grumbolt expertly drove the Cob Car through the streets. A few cheered.

"Take the next left, to approach the main gates of the Diorama Desert."

Grumbolt hung a left. And indeed, he did see the gates. He also saw loops.

SIX.
GIANT.
LOOPS.

CHAPTER TWENTY-SIX
ROUTE LOOPS

Six gigantic mega death loops. And the last one was on fire for some reason. They were put there to dissuade toys from trying to enter the dangerous Diorama Desert. Grumbolt hit the brakes.

"Uh, any alternate plans that don't involve loops?" Key Bee asked.

"No," Grumbolt said. "Key Bee, you did great. But now I have to ask you to fly away from the car."

Key Bee fluttered out of the car. "But the loops!—You're scared of them!"

She was right. Grumbolt was frightened.

But the only way to save Toy World, the only way to deliver the bears someplace they couldn't hurt anyone, was to complete all six loops.

The cotton in Grumbolt's stomach was flip-flopping at the thought of taking on one loop, let alone six. And he hit the gas anyway.

Grumbolt
entered the loops.

No time to celebrate, though. The second loop went really, really high and then super curved. The fourth loop went really, really high and then avoid numerous signs like, TURN BACK NOW And the sixth loop *was worse.*

He took the first loop, which really wasn't that bad!

loop was *much* higher . . . It ended with a ramp, which propelled Grumbolt to the third loop, which was

really, really low. The fifth loop was easy: Grumbolt just had to

and SERIOUSLY IT'S ABOUT TO GET WORSE.

It was on FIRE.

But Grumbolt avoided the flames, and *completed the loops*.

All that remained was a relatively quiet patch of road before the main gates of the Diorama Desert. The bears CRASHED THROUGH THE LOOPS, still in hot pursuit.

Grumbolt plowed through the gates. He felt the desert's searing heat immediately. The steering wheel began to melt between his paws. The tires popped as the back of the Cob Car started smoking.

The legion of eager Teddy Bears was closing in.

CHAPTER TWENTY-SEVEN
EMBRACE YOUR DESTINY

The Cob Car let out one last wheeze before dying. Grumbolt climbed out.

The bears were sluggish from the heat, but still eager to hug.

He stretched his arms out, threw his head back, and yelled, "Let's do this!"

The bears scooped him up and squeezed. Grumbolt hugged each and every one. Fuzzy bears, velvet bears, patchwork bears, even that darn Get Well Soon Bear.

Grumbolt's stitches began to pop.
But the bears kept hugging.

CHAPTER TWENTY-EIGHT
ALL'S WELL THAT ENDS NOW

OmniBus Squared pulled up to the entrance of the Diorama Desert. The surviving members of Elite Action Force Now followed, with Tempest and Braino held in their Ultra Helicopter.

Commander Hedgehog, Micro, and Rex got off the old yellow bus.

Key Bee joined them and told them about Grumbolt's plan.

"He went into the desert?" Micro said, worried. "With *them* . . ."

"He's a true action hero," Rex said. "That loser is a total winner."

"Yes, that little guy, Gumball, was an adequate sidekick to Rex," General Elite said. "He'll make a fine footnote in our history, but he's gone. Now, let's seal up Diorama Desert's main gates so the bears can't return."

"We're not doing that!" Micro said. "Grumbolt is still out there!"

Commander Hedgehog agreed. "What do you suggest we do?"

Micro was ready. "We get a search and rescue team in ASAP. It'll be hot. OmniBus, reach out to all available water- and/or ice-based action figures."

"I can run in now!" Rex said. "I can run super fast and find him."

As Micro tried to deduce which Elite Action Force Now vehicle would survive the longest in the desert, Tempest decided she had had enough. She reeled back and slammed her battle glove against the helicopter door. It flew off . . . and Tempest marched toward the gates.

Elite Action Force Now aimed their accessories at her.

"I am made of ultra-polycarbonate," Tempest said. "Superplastic. I will last slightly longer than any of you in the desert heat."

"She's right," Micro said. "But the heat is so strong, superplastic or no, you'll melt quickly."

"If I melt, I'll melt a hero!" Tempest said, running into the Diorama Desert.

Three minutes went by.

And then five.

Around minute ten, Micro, Rex, and Key Bee were ready to go into the desert to see if they could help. The members of Elite Action Force Now were trying to find a polite way to leave and resume their anniversary celebration.

And then.

A figure stumbled out from the gates.

It was Tempest. She had not melted, having gotten out in the nick of time. But she was weak, tired . . .

. . . and holding a tiny, misshapen, slightly torn but very heroic Grumbolt in her arms.

"I found him alone in the desert," Tempest said.

"Grumbolt, you fought the bears?" Rex asked.

Grumbolt smiled.

"I hugged them. They hugged back. And then, I just started giving really bad hugs. Limp, weak embraces that kind of annoyed the bears. They finally dropped me and headed off to find someone else."

Tempest placed an exhausted Grumbolt on the ground. Micro and Rex ran over and helped him up. Micro went to embrace him.

"I love you, Micro, but no hugging for a little while." Grumbolt sighed. "I'm all hugged out."

And with that, Commander Hedgehog and his students began their drive back to Toy Academy. OmniBus took the long way, to avoid any loops. Everyone had had enough action for one day.

CHAPTER TWENTY-NINE
ONE MONTH LATER

Grumbolt's Cob Car zoomed through the triple-loop racetrack. Rex cheered from the passenger seat.

"Yes! Faster! Faster!"

Grumbolt was glad Rex had agreed to let them use the rebuilt Cob Car for the Obstacle Course midterm. After all, the commander was nice enough to retrieve the Cob Car from the desert, and Micro was nice enough to rebuild it. Besides, Grumbolt was used to this car. It was *his* car.

The loops, of course, were no problem. After you've driven on six obstacle-laden loops while being chased by a herd of Teddy Bears, driving up three bearless loops is actually kind of boring. They completed the driving part of the Obstacle Course midterm with the highest score in the class.

"Yes, we did it!" Grumbolt said. "That'll make up for completely bungling the first two parts of the midterm, which we didn't prepare for at all."

Rex headed over to his van and patted it on the hood. He wanted to make sure it wasn't jealous. "By the way, Grumbolt, you're welcome I carried you through those."

Grumbolt smiled. "You're welcome I saved you and everyone else at Toy Academy from a giant bear attack. Come on, let's go see how Micro and Key Bee are doing."

Micro sat in the passenger seat as Key Bee drove the Rocket Cycle. Micro had a newfound appreciation for her sidekick. After all, Key Bee had helped Grumbolt lead the bears out of town. Like Grumbolt, she had received a key to the city as a thank you from President Space Lincoln. It was officially Key Bee's favorite key. And she was never, ever letting go of it.

Which made it impossible to drive well.

They flew off the track into the science building, which collapsed again.

Toy Academy's newest students watched from the bleachers.

"I'm glad that since we just enrolled, they didn't make us do the obstacle course," Braino stated. "Also, I'm glad they didn't arrest us. When all was said and done, you *did* help out."

Tempest nodded. "We are going to be the greatest toys and the greatest heroes in this or any other world. We just have to learn."

"I'm not going to learn anything from my classes," Braino said. "I'm already the smartest toy here."

Tempest shook her head. "You're the second smartest. That space-girl with the breakfast-danish hairstyle is way smarter. Besides, I never said we're going to learn from classes. We're going to learn how to be a hero by *watching a true hero.*"

She peered through her binoculars and zeroed in on Grumbolt.

"Teach me your ways . . . " she said quietly to herself.

After class, Grumbolt sat with Micro, Rex, and Key Bee outside of Castle Fort Lair. All of them had passed the Obstacle Course, and none of them had done it exceptionally well.

"It's okay," Micro said. "That's why we're in school. Lots to learn."

There was a long silence. Grumbolt knew it was coming.

"Next semester, though," Micro said. "Next semester I'm gonna do it perfectly. You guys are, too. I'm gonna make sure of it."

Grumbolt and Rex exchanged looks. This did not sound fun.

"Talk to her," Rex said. "She's your friend."

Grumbolt shrugged. "She's yours, too."

To everyone's surprise, including his own, Rex Everything didn't argue this.

They looked out at Toy Academy. Hundreds of toys, of all shapes, sizes, and materials, hurried to class. There were plushes; there were collectables. There were water toys, squeaky toys, robots, racing cars, and action figures.

And none of them, not a single one, had their stuffing together.

BRIAN LYNCH is a screenwriter whose work includes the movies *Minions*, *Puss in Boots*, *Hop*, *The Secret Life of Pets*, and *The Secret Life of Pets 2*. He has also written the comic books *Monster Motors*, *Bill & Ted's Most Triumphant Return*, *Spike*, and *Angel: After the Fall*. He currently lives in Los Angeles with his wife and son. He firmly believes that the greatest toy is either a 1982 Dakin stuffed dog puppet or a *Masters of the Universe* Wave 3 Orko figurine.

EDWARDIAN TAYLOR works as a freelance Visual Development Artist for mobile games, TV, films, and commercials in Dallas, Texas. He is also the illustrator of the picture books *Race!*, written by Sue Fliess, and *It's Not Jack and the Beanstalk*, written by Josh Funk. Learn more about him at edwardiantaylor.com and follow him on Twitter, Instagram and Tumblr @edwardiantaylor.